Walt Disney

Winnie the Pooh

Twin Books

One fine autumn day, Winnie the Pooh sat on a log in front of his house in the Hundred-Acre Wood. Something seemed to be wrong. Instead of his usual smile, Pooh Bear was wearing a frown and scratching his head.

"Think, think, think. Whatever can be wrong?" said Pooh. He was a bear of little brain, so thinking was sometimes hard for him. Beside him lay four of his honey pots, and all of them were empty. "That's it! I'm hungry, but I have eaten all of my honey. Oh, bother," sighed Pooh, wandering back inside his house.

Noisily pulling more empty jars out of the cupboard, Pooh stuck his paw in one of them. "There's a bit left in this one, but hardly enough for a hungry bear like me," he said as he licked off the honey.

Just as his tummy began to rumble with hunger, Pooh heard a buzzing sound. Turning around, he saw a bee fly in through the window.

"A bee," thought Pooh Bear. "Now what do bees do? They make honey. And the only reason bees make honey is so I can eat it!" With a smile on his face, he followed the bee outside and watched it fly up into a tree.

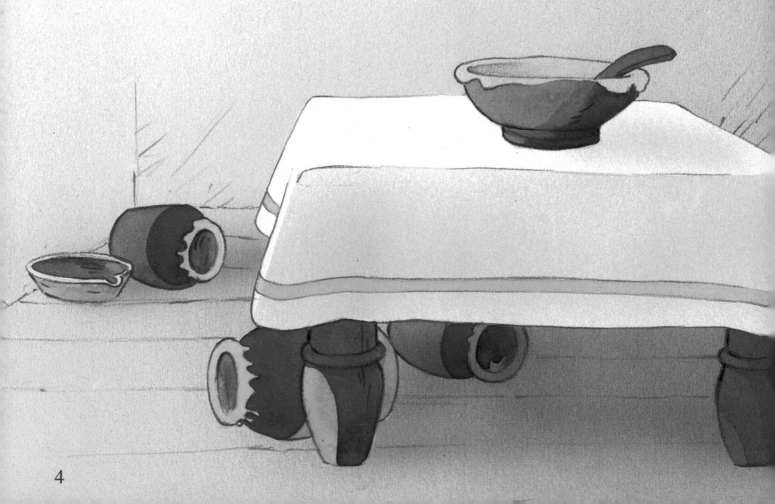

"Now, if I can just follow that bee, he's bound to lead me to honey," said Winnie the Pooh as he began to climb the very tall tree. Finally, Pooh reached the spot where the bee had disappeared. But just as he was about to stick his paw into the hole, the branch he was climbing on broke in half and Pooh began to fall.

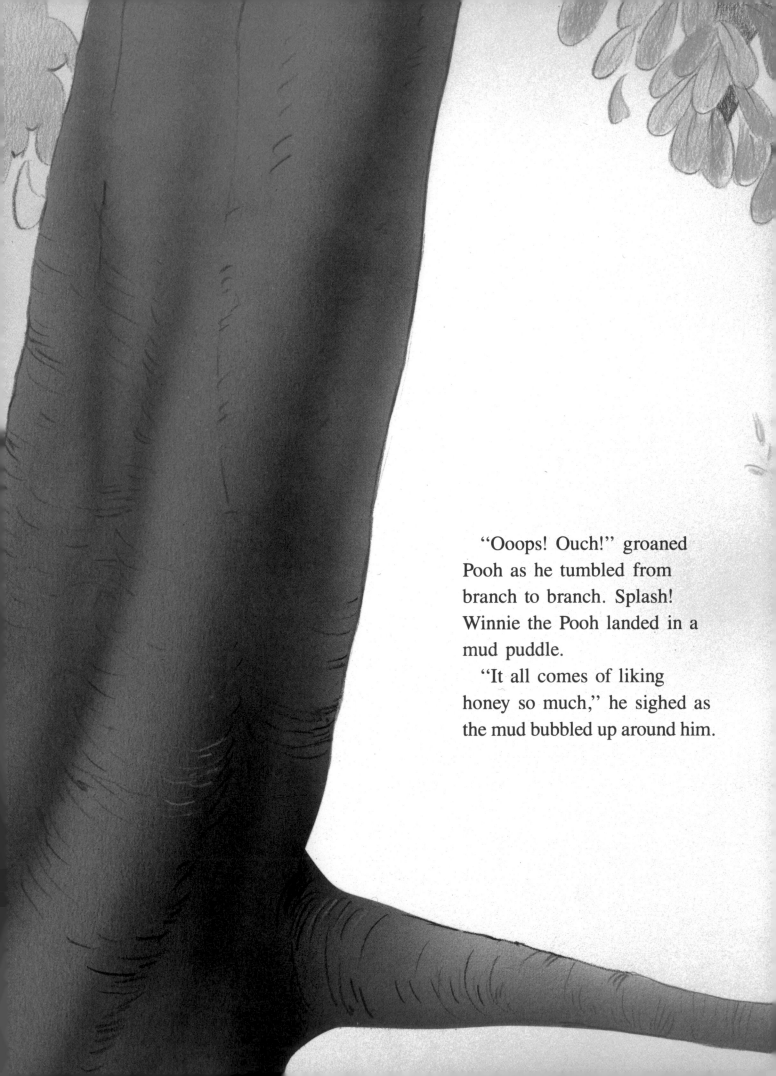

"Ooops! Ouch!" groaned Pooh as he tumbled from branch to branch. Splash! Winnie the Pooh landed in a mud puddle.

"It all comes of liking honey so much," he sighed as the mud bubbled up around him.

Not far away, at the edge of the forest, lived Christopher Robin. He was a good friend to all the animals. Always willing to lend a hand, the boy was busy that day helping out poor Eeyore, the donkey, who had lost his tail.

"Now, Eeyore, I'm going to nail your tail back on. Try not to lose it again," said Christopher Robin, as he knelt down behind the donkey. Kanga and Owl stood nearby, watching.

"A bit to the left," suggested Kanga.

"No, absolutely not," said Owl. "Move it to the right." When Christopher Robin had finished, Eeyore gave his tail a mighty swish.

"Thanks," he said. "It's just an old tail, but I'm kind of attached to it."

Just as the animals and Christopher Robin were congratulating one another, along came Winnie the Pooh.

"Hello, Pooh Bear. What have you been up to now?" asked Christopher Robin, looking down at his muddy friend.

"Hello, Christopher Robin. I was just wondering, uh, just thinking about whether you had such a thing as a balloon?"

Christopher Robin was puzzled. "What do you want a balloon for?" he asked.

Winnie the Pooh looked around and whispered, "Honey."

"But you don't get honey with a balloon," Christopher Robin pointed out.

"I do," insisted Pooh. As
Christopher Robin went to get
a balloon, Pooh rolled over
and over in another puddle
until he was completely
covered with mud. Then he
took the balloon from
Christopher Robin and began
floating slowly upward.

"I'll be able to reach the
bee's nest with this," he
explained.

"But the bees will see you,"
shouted Christopher Robin.

"Yes, but with this mud all
over me, they'll think I'm a
little black rain cloud,"
laughed Winnie the Pooh as
he floated higher and higher.

Christopher Robin followed along below, as the breezes blew Pooh Bear toward the honey tree. When he drifted close enough to the hole, he reached in and pulled out a paw full of honey.

"Yum! Yum! Nothing like fresh honey," said Pooh, dripping honey everywhere. A swarm of angry bees flew out of the nest and buzzed threateningly around him.

"Christopher Robin!" shouted Winnie the Pooh. "I think the bees suspect something."

"They probably think that you're after their honey!" the boy shouted back.

By this time a whole swarm of bees buzzed angrily
around Pooh.

"Christopher Robin, I have come to the conclusion that
these are not the right sort of bees," said Pooh, slapping
away the angry insects. "No, not at all a nice sort of bee,"
he proclaimed, as a bee stung his nose.

As Pooh perched himself unsteadily on top of the drifting balloon, the swarm of bees suddenly attacked. Soon, Pooh heard a loud hissing noise as air began to escape from the balloon.

"Christopher Robin!" called Winnie the Pooh. "I think I will come down now."

"Don't worry, Pooh Bear," said the boy. Christopher Robin ran with outstretched arms and caught Pooh just before he reached the ground. "Silly old bear," laughed the boy.

"Oh, dear," sighed Pooh. "If only I didn't like honey so much."

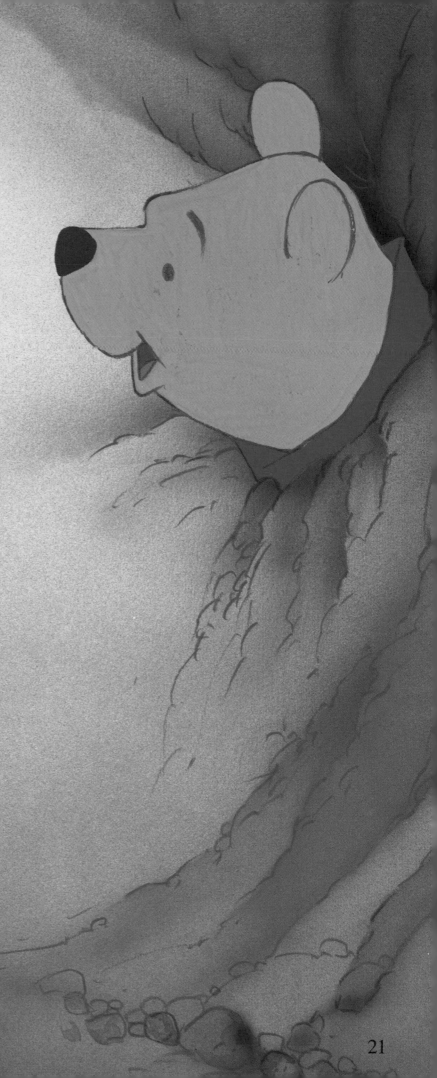

But Winnie the Pooh was not one to give up easily. As soon as his bee stings were better, he had another idea.

"Honey rhymes with bunny!" thought Pooh. "I think I'll go pay Rabbit a visit."

Rabbit was just about to pour himself a cup of tea when Pooh popped his head into the rabbit hole. "Anybody at home?" he shouted.

The startled Rabbit spilled his tea. "Oh, no. Not Pooh," he thought in alarm. "He'll eat me out of house and home." But Pooh kept calling and Rabbit realized he couldn't avoid the hungry bear. "How about lunch?" asked Rabbit.

"Thank you, Rabbit. I am feeling a bit hungry," said Pooh, making himself at home.

Rabbit brought out a jar of honey. "Would you like some honey on your bread?" he asked.

"Don't bother about the bread. I'll just take a tiny helping of honey," said Winnie the Pooh, tying a napkin around his neck.

Rabbit poured out a small helping of honey. Pooh's face fell when he saw the tiny golden dot.

"What's wrong?" asked Rabbit.

"Well, I did mean a somewhat larger tiny helping," Pooh admitted.

23

Rabbit handed Pooh the jar. "Perhaps you should just help yourself," he said.

Winnie the Pooh began eating honey. As soon as he finished one jar, he started on another. He ate and ate and ate until he was nearly covered with honey. Then he turned to Rabbit and said, "Thanks so much. I think I'll be going now."

Rabbit looked at Pooh's large tummy, which was now even larger than usual. "You're sure you won't have any more?"

Pooh looked around at the empty jars. "*Is* there any more?" he asked.

"No, there isn't," answered Rabbit, shaking Pooh's sticky paw.

Licking his paws, Pooh started to leave. Suddenly, Rabbit heard a muffled shout. "Help! I'm stuck!" Sure enough, Pooh Bear was wedged in the entrance to Rabbit's house!

"That's what happens when you eat too much," he said, giving Pooh a push from behind.

"No," replied Pooh. "This is what happens when you make your door too small."

Rabbit pushed and Pooh struggled, but he was still stuck.

Pooh was wedged in the hole so tightly that he didn't budge an inch. Finally, he began to yell for help. Soon Owl arrived. "Well, if it isn't Winnie the Pooh!"

"Hello, Owl," replied Pooh.

"Are you, by any chance, stuck?" asked Owl.

"Oh, no. Just resting and thinking, that's all," replied the bear.

"Yes. I'd say you were definitely in a tight spot," said Owl, taking a closer look.

29

Back inside his house,
Rabbit was staring at Pooh's
rear end. "Oh, dear. Oh,
gracious. If I have to look at
that—that thing for some time,
I might as well make the best
of it," he muttered.

Rabbit placed branches on
either side of Pooh's bottom
and put a frame around it.

"A hunting trophy!" he
exclaimed, stepping back to
admire his work.

That night, Pooh was still wedged in the hole when a gopher stopped by. "I hear there's an excavation problem here. My name's Gopher and here's my card. What's the problem?"

"I'm the problem," sighed Pooh. "I'm stuck in this doorway."

Gopher dusted off the bear and tied a scarf around his head. "Looks as if this may take several days," he said, opening his lunch box.

"Several days!" gulped Pooh. "What about meals?"

"No thanks. I've brought mine with me," replied the gopher as he began to eat.

Later that night, Gopher realized it would be very difficult to unwedge Pooh. Staying only long enough to eat up the last few crumbs of his food, the gopher packed up and left.

"Oh, bother," yawned Pooh Bear. "If only I didn't like honey so much, this never would have happened."

When Christopher Robin learned of Pooh Bear's predicament, he came running to help. After much thought, the boy decided that the only solution was for Winnie the Pooh to lose weight.

"We're going to put you on a diet, Pooh," said Christopher Robin. "And a diet means NO HONEY!" he declared firmly.

Finally, as Rabbit was beginning to give up on ever using his front door again, Pooh began to budge. Christopher Robin, Kanga and Eeyore tugged on Pooh from outside while Rabbit pushed from the inside.

And with a hearty heave-ho, Pooh was free at last!

Several days later, as Winnie the Pooh strolled through the Hundred-Acre Wood, a great wind lifted him right off his feet.

"Oh, goodness. I must have lost a lot of weight. I feel as light as a feather," said the surprised bear. And like a feather, Winnie the Pooh was swept up through the trees.

It was a very blustery day
and the wind was blowing
harder every minute.

As he swirled above the
ground, Pooh heard a familiar
voice. Looking ahead, he saw
his friend Piglet.

"Piglet! Wait for me!"
shouted Pooh as he reached
out and grabbed Piglet's scarf.

Just then, a strong wind
separated the two friends. As
Pooh Bear went flying up
toward the tree where Owl
lived, Piglet hung onto a
branch with all his might.

Owl poked his head out of
the door. "Nice of you to
drop in, Winnie the Pooh," he
said. "Oh, and I see you've
brought Piglet with you. Well,
do come in."

41

As Pooh and Piglet sat in Owl's house, they could feel the house swaying from side to side. Owl, in his rocking chair, didn't seem to notice. He was too busy telling them a long story about his relatives.

"I say, Owl," said Pooh. "The house appears to be moving."

"Nonsense," declared Owl. "This house is as solid as a rock. It'll take more than a little breeze to blow it away."

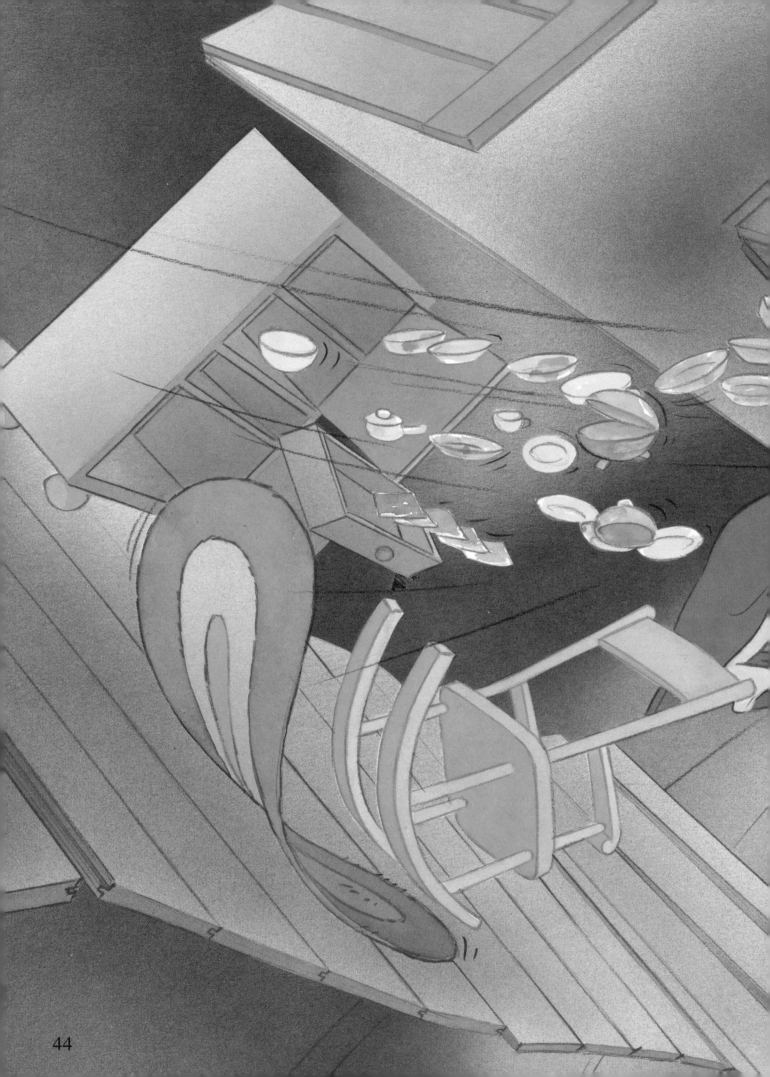

Just as Owl said this, an enormous gust of wind blew the roof off. Owl's cupboard doors flew open and plates and saucers came tumbling out. Before anyone could say a word, Pooh Bear, Piglet and Owl were all blown out of the house.

Pooh found his way home
and hopped into his warm,
snuggly bed. But the night
was filled with strange noises.
One of those noises had never
been heard before. Pooh,
being a bear of very little
brain, decided to invite the
new sound in. He gathered up
his courage and his popgun
and went to the door.

Winnie the Pooh opened the door and peered out
cautiously. He couldn't see anything. But then, before he
knew what had hit him, a large creature with black stripes
bounced on top of him, knocking him over.

"Hello! I'm Tigger," said the creature, looking down at
Pooh. "That's spelled T-I-double G-RRRR. Tigger. What's
your name?"

"My name is Winnie the Pooh, and you scared me,"
answered Pooh.

"Of course I scared you. Tiggers are supposed to be scary,"
replied the bouncy tiger, who really wasn't scary at all.

"The wonderful thing about Tiggers is I'm the only one!" Tigger continued.

"Then what's that over there?" asked Pooh, pointing toward the mirror.

Tigger bounced over to the mirror. "What a funny-looking creature," he laughed. Seeing his mirror image laughing, Tigger said, "I'll teach that animal to laugh at me." He growled at the tiger in the mirror. But when the tiger in the mirror growled back, Tigger became so frightened, he bounced right out of Pooh's house.

Pooh thought he should stay awake and keep watch for other strange creatures, like Heffalumps and Woozles, but he was so tired, he fell asleep.

He had a very strange dream about honey and Heffalumps and Woozles and as he dreamed, a heavy rain began to fall.

The strange dream soon turned into a nightmare. Just as he dreamed he was drowning in honey, Pooh Bear woke up and found himself in a puddle, but not of honey. There was water everywhere.

"Oh, no! My honey!" yelled Pooh. "I mustn't let the water get into my honey jars."

Pooh quickly carried all of
his precious honey jars to
safety up in the big tree above
his house.

The rain continued to fall,
and the Hundred-Acre Wood
got wetter and wetter until it
turned into a huge lake.

All the climbing had made Pooh a bit hungry. "I'll just have a little something," he said as he poked his nose into one of the jars.

While Pooh was busy eating honey, the water continued to rise all the way up to the branch where the bear sat.

A sudden wave of water knocked Pooh over, headfirst, into the honey jar. He was quite a sight with his legs kicking in the air.

Floating nearby was Piglet, who was sailing on a kitchen chair. "Is that you, Winnie the Pooh?" shouted Piglet. "It's me, Piglet! Can you hear me?"

Piglet was too busy trying to get Pooh's attention to notice a waterfall up ahead. Both Pooh and Piglet cried out in alarm, but there was nothing they could do. They plunged down the roaring waterfall, tumbling over and over as they were tossed about by the falling water. When they landed safely in the river below, Pooh was floating on the kitchen chair and Piglet was inside the honey jar.

Luckily, Christopher Robin had been looking for his little friends, and he soon had the waterlogged bear and piglet safe on dry land.

"You rescued Piglet," Christopher Robin told Pooh. "You are a hero."

Once the flood waters had receded, Christopher Robin had a Hero Party for Pooh. He invited Rabbit, Kanga and little Roo, Piglet, Pooh and even Tigger.

Owl made a speech about Pooh's bravery and everything seemed to be back to normal— at least for the moment.

Several weeks later, while Rabbit was picking carrots in his garden, Tigger happened to bounce by.

"Oh, no!" groaned Rabbit when he saw Tigger bouncing in his cabbage patch. With every energetic bounce, Tigger smashed, scattered or squashed some of Rabbit's favorite vegetables.

"Hello, Rabbit!" shouted Tigger.

Rabbit looked around at the scattered vegetables. "Tigger, just look at what you've done to my beautiful garden!" he shouted, waving his fist.

"Yuck! Messy, isn't it?" said Tigger, looking around him.

"You've ruined it, Tigger. It's your doing. You and your confounded bouncing! Oh, why don't you ever stop bouncing?" the angry Rabbit demanded.

"Bouncing is what Tiggers do best," Tigger answered. So Rabbit turned to Piglet and Winnie the Pooh.

"I'm going to teach that Tigger a lesson," he said. "Let's take him for a long walk in the woods and lose him."

"Lose him?" asked Pooh.

"Oh, we'll find him again the next morning. But it will take the bounce out of him," answered Rabbit.

The next morning, they set off into the forest. As usual, Tigger bounced ahead of everyone.

After a while, the three friends managed to lose Tigger, who bounced off into the misty forest. After waiting some time to be sure that Tigger was truly out of sight, Rabbit nudged Pooh and Piglet and they turned toward home. However, the mist had thickened and everything looked different than before.

"You know, Rabbit," said Pooh Bear, "I don't think we lost Tigger. I think he lost us."

Tigger got home before his friends. And so it was that the lesson Rabbit wanted to teach Tigger backfired.

When the first snowfall covered the Hundred-Acre Wood, little Roo waited anxiously for Tigger to come and take him out to play.

"Now, you be careful, dear," said Roo's mother Kanga when Tigger arrived. "And bring Roo home in time for his nap," she shouted as Tigger and Roo bounced off in the snow.

Tigger and Roo reached the frozen pond.

"Can you ice skate, Tigger?" asked Roo.

"Sure! Ice skating is what Tiggers do best!" bragged
Tigger as he glided across the ice.

Soon Tigger was doing figure eights and even skating
backward while Roo cheered him on.

Tigger began to make more daring moves. He was so busy showing off, he didn't even see Rabbit in front of him.

"Oh, no! Not you!" screamed Rabbit as Tigger came spinning toward him, out of control.

"Look out!" shouted Tigger. "Out of my way! I can't . . ." as he banged right into Rabbit " . . . stop!" Poor Rabbit was sent flying through a snowbank and into his own house.

"Yuck! Tiggers hate ice skating," said Tigger, as he and Roo bounced into the woods.

"Can you climb a tree, Tigger?" asked Roo.

"Climb a tree? Why, that's what Tiggers do best. Only I don't climb trees—I bounce them."

With Roo holding onto his shoulders, Tigger bounced from limb to limb of a tall tree. Higher and higher he bounced, until he was as high as he could go.

The last bounce was too much for Roo, who fell off his friend's shoulders. On the way down, Roo grabbed onto Tigger's tail and began to swing back and forth. "This is fun," he shouted. "I've never swung on a tiger's tail before."

"Hey! Stop that, please! You're rocking the forest," said Tigger, as the tree began to sway dangerously.

Roo let go of Tigger's tail and landed on a lower branch. "What's wrong, Tigger?" he asked.

"Oh, thank goodness! I was getting seasick," answered Tigger.

Just then Pooh and Piglet spotted Tigger.

"Helloooo!" shouted the tiger.

"Why, it's Tigger and Roo," said Pooh. "What are you two doing up there?" he shouted.

"We bounced up. But now Tigger is stuck," said Roo.

Soon Kanga and Rabbit
arrived to see what all the
shouting was about.

"Oh, dear!" exclaimed
Kanga. "Well, do be careful,
Roo, and jump into my apron.
I'll catch you. But try not to
fall too fast," said Kanga, as
she got ready to catch Roo.

"Whee! That was fun,"
giggled Roo, leaping down
and landing in his mother's
apron.

"Okay, you're next!" Pooh and Rabbit shouted to Tigger. "Jump!"

"Tiggers don't jump. They bounce!" said Tigger, holding on tightly to the tree.

"Then bounce down," said Pooh.

"Don't be ridiculous," said Tigger. "Tiggers don't bounce down. They bounce up!"

"Then climb down," shouted Rabbit impatiently.

"Tiggers don't climb down, because—because—their tails get in the way," answered Tigger, wrapping his tail around the tree.

"That settles it," said Rabbit, who was actually enjoying Tigger's predicament. "If he won't jump or climb down, he'll have to stay up there forever."

"Forever!" yelled Tigger. "Oh, I promise if I ever get down from this tree, I'll never bounce again. Never!"

Rabbit was thrilled. "Did you hear that, everyone?" he asked, gleefully. "He promised. He said never!"

The friends decided that the best way to get Tigger down was for him to slide. So slowly and cautiously, with their encouragement, Tigger slid down the tree.

"You can open your eyes now. You're safe," said Piglet as Tigger reached the bottom of the tree.

Tigger was so happy to be back on the ground, he started to kiss the snow. "I'm so happy, I feel like bouncing!" he said, and he immediately began to bounce.

"Wait a minute. You promised, Tigger," said Rabbit.

Tigger sat down. "I did? You mean I can never bounce again? Not even one teeny bounce?"

Rabbit and the others shook their heads. Tigger sighed and sat on a nearby log. There was a long, sad silence.

"I like the old bouncy Tigger best," said little Roo.

"So do we," agreed Kanga and Piglet.

"Of course. We all do," added Winnie the Pooh. "Don't you agree, Rabbit?"

"Well, ah, oh, all right," muttered Rabbit, with great reluctance. "I guess I like the old bouncy Tigger best."

"Oh, boy," said Tigger, bouncing right on top of Rabbit. "Come on. I'll teach you all how to bounce." Soon, Tigger and the others—including Rabbit—bounced off into the snowy Hundred-Acre Wood together.

Produced by
Twin Books,
15 Sherwood Place,
Greenwich, CT 08630

ISBN 1 85469 989 X

Reprinted in 1992

Printed in Hong Kong